The DRAGONLING

4 books in 1!

The DRAGONLING

4 books in 1!

The Dragonling

A Dragon in the Family

Dragon Quest

Dragons of Krad

By Jackie French Koller

Illustrated by Judith Mitchell

New Yo w Delhi

ALADDIN

An imprint of Simon & Schuster Children's Publishing Division

1230 Avenue of the Americas, New York, New York 10020

This Aladdin hardcover edition April 2019

The Dragonling text copyright © 1990 by Jackie French Koller

A Dragon in the Family text copyright © 1993 by Jackie French Koller

Dragon Quest text and interior illustrations copyright © 1997 by Jackie French Koller

Dragons of Krad text copyright © 1997 by Jackie French Koller

Cover illustration copyright © 2018 by Tom Knight

The Dragonling interior illustrations copyright © 1990 by Judith Mitchell

A Dragon in the Family interior illustrations copyright © 1993 by Judith Mitchell

Dragons of Krad interior illustrations copyright © 1997 by Judith Mitchell

For information about special discounts for bulk purchases, please contact Simon & Schuster Special Sales at 1-866-506-1949 or business@simonandschuster.com.

The Simon & Schuster Speakers Bureau can bring authors to your live event. For more information or to book an event contact the Simon & Schuster Speakers Bureau at 1-866-248-3049 or visit our website at www.simonspeakers.com.

Series designed by Laura Lyn DiSiena

The text of this book was set in ITC New Baskerville.

Manufactured in the United States of America 0319 FFG

2 4 6 8 10 9 7 5 3 1

Library of Congress Control Number 2019931735

ISBN 978-1-5344-5395-1 (hc)

ISBN 978-1-5344-0063-4 (*The Dragonling* eBook)

ISBN 978-1-5344-0066-5 (*A Dragon in the Family* eBook)

ISBN 978-1-5344-0069-6 (*Dragon Quest* eBook)

ISBN 978-1-5344-0072-6 (*Dragons of Krad* eBook)

These titles were previously published individually.

CONTENTS

The Dragonling

To Devin, because dragons are his
second-favorite animal, next to dogs

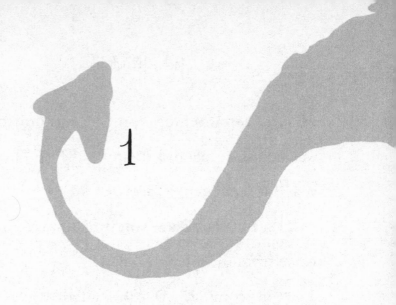

1

DAREK AWOKE AT THE FIRST LIGHT
of dawn. He sat up quickly and pushed his bed
curtains aside. Through his window he could see
the soft violet rays of the morning sun just touch-
ing the tips of the yellow mountains of Orr. His
brother, Clep, was up there somewhere, probably
breaking camp, getting ready for the day's hunt. It
wasn't fair, Darek thought. Why did he have to wait
three more years before *his* first dragonquest? So

what if Clep was twelve and he was only nine. He was nearly as tall and strong as Clep. Three more years! It seemed like forever.

"Darek? Darek, are you up?" It was his mother's voice from the kitchen below.

"I'm coming," Darek called back. He got dressed and clattered down the stairs.

His mother was bent over the hearth, spooning porridge into his bowl. Darek slid into his place at the table.

"Do you think maybe the men will be home today?" he asked.

His mother's brow wrinkled with worry as she served him his breakfast.

"Who knows how long they will be gone?" she said. "Ten days? Twenty? A dragonquest ends when it ends."

"I can't wait until it's my turn," Darek said eagerly. "I will be the one to make the kill. I will win the claws to wear around my neck. I will be the Marksman, like Father."

Darek's mother shook her head and turned back to the fire.

"Why are you silent, Mother?" Darek asked. "Why don't you get excited about the dragonquest like everyone else?"

"My brother was killed on his first dragonquest," said Darek's mother quietly.

"Many have been killed on the dragonquests," said Darek, "but they are heroes. You should be proud."

Darek's mother sighed. "In the old days," she said, "when the dragons were plentiful, when they threatened the villages and raided the yuke* herds,

*yuke: a white, long-haired animal, much like a goat, only larger

that was the time for heroes. Now the dragons are few, and they keep to the mountains. Why should we send young boys into their midst?"

"They are not boys," said Darek. "They are men, and they must face a dragon to prove it."

"There are other ways to prove you are a man," said Darek's mother.

"What are they, then?" asked Darek.

"Doing your work with pride, caring for others, and thinking your own thoughts are good ways," said Darek's mother.

"*Bah,*" said Darek. "Anyone can do those things, but only a man can slay a dragon."

There was a sudden, loud clanging, and Darek's mother's head jerked up.

"The men return," she said.

Darek and his mother ran to the village square.

The hunting party was threading its way down through the mountain pass, pulling a great wagon. Upon it lay a hulking mound.

"A Blue!" shouted Darek. "It's a Great Blue!" Great Blues were the largest and fiercest of all dragons. Darek could hardly contain his excitement as he raced to meet the party. But as he drew closer, his steps faltered. He could see that his father was leading a yuke, and slung over the yuke's saddle was a small body, about the size of Clep's. Darek heard his mother cry out behind him.

Other children jostled Darek as they rushed by. "What's the matter? Hurry up! Get out of the way!" Darek swallowed hard and tried to ignore the great weight that had settled in his chest. If it *was* Clep, he must be brave. He must not shed a tear. He must be honored to have a hero for a brother.

Then a voice called out. "Darek! Mother! Over here!" A yuke broke out of the hunting party, and Darek saw that its rider was Clep. Relief rushed over him as he ran to meet his brother.

Clep swung himself down out of the saddle. He held up a necklace. A necklace made of claws! "I made the kill!" he shouted. "I killed a Great Blue!"

Darek fought back a pang of jealousy. "I can't believe it!" he shouted, thumping Clep on the back. "You? The Marksman!"

Darek's mother came up beside them. There was joy and relief in her eyes as she hugged Clep tightly to her, but when he held up the blood-stained necklace, she looked away.

"Who is the fallen one?" she asked quietly.

Clep's face grew grave. "It is Yoran," he said.

The weight came back to Darek's chest. Yoran?

Clep's best friend? Yoran, who had been like a second brother in their house ever since Darek could remember? Yoran, who ran faster than the wind? How could it be he who lay so still now across the saddle?

Darek's mother nodded, her face like stone. "I must go to his mother," she said.

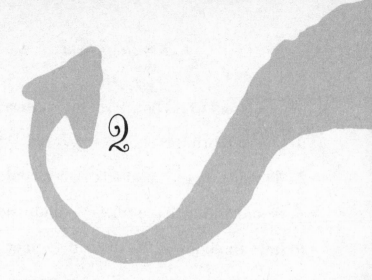

2

DAREK COULDN'T SLEEP. HE WAS TOO
excited about the festival tomorrow. His brother,
Clep, and all their family would be the guests of
honor. There would be dancing and feasting, and
then at night a great bonfire in which the body of
the dragon would be burned. Now it lay on the
wagon, just outside the paddock fence. Tomorrow
night its ashes would be placed in a carved urn and
given to Clep. Clep would place the urn on the

mantel, next to his father's. One day Darek vowed to place an urn there too.

Outside, in the paddock, Darek could hear the nervous rustling of the yukes. It made them uneasy to have the body of the dragon so near. Darek listened. The house was still. No one would know if he went down to comfort Nonni, his favorite, and gave her a bit of sugar. He crept out in his nightshirt.

"Here, Nonni, little pet," he whispered. The small yuke ran to his side and nuzzled him gently. Darek took the sugar from his pocket and fed it to her. Her rough, wet tongue tickled his hand as she licked every crumb from between his fingers.

Darek stared at the great dragon. He could see it clearly in the light of Zoriak's twin moons. It lay on its side, its wings twisted and crumpled, its once-fearsome claws stubby and blunt. Darek got goose bumps thinking about how it must have looked in life. He walked around it, imagining it standing on its powerful legs, flames shooting from its mouth. He could see it charge. He could hear it roar. He could hear it . . . whimper?

Darek jumped back. He was sure he had heard something. Could the creature still be alive? Darek wasn't taking any chances. He dived for cover behind a barliberry bush and lay still, waiting. The sound came again, *huf-uh huf-uh,* a soft hiccuping kind of sob. Darek peeked out. The great head lay just in front of him, still as death. He crept out of hiding and circled the creature once again. Then he saw it—a tiny head peeking out of the pouch on the giant dragon's belly. *A dragonling!*

Darek stared in amazement. He knew dragons

carried their young in pouches until they were old enough to fend for themselves, but he had never seen a live dragonling before. The small creature came out of the pouch and climbed unsteadily up its mother's chest. It was about half as big as Darek, and he guessed it to be very young, maybe even newborn.

The dragonling licked its mother's still face with its forked tongue, whimpering all the while. Darek stepped back and slipped on a pebble, falling to the ground. The dragonling twisted its neck and looked at him, its eyes shining pale green in the night.

"Rrronk," it said, and began to climb down in his direction.

Darek scrambled to his feet. Small as the creature was, it was still a dragon, and Darek had no wish to face it unarmed. He picked up a big stick. The dragonling fluttered down off the wagon and approached on wobbly legs.

"*Rrronk,*" it said again.

Darek held the stick out like a sword. The dragonling stopped and sniffed it. It gave it a lick, then whimpered again. Darek had been taught all his life to hate and fear dragons, but it was hard to hate such a small one, and an orphan at that. He lowered his club, and the dragonling came up and nuzzled him.

Darek felt in his pocket. There was a small lump of sugar left. He held it out cautiously. The little dragon sniffed it, then the forked tongue flicked out, and it was gone.

"*Thrrrummmm,*" said the dragon. It was a happy sound. The dragon nuzzled him again.

"I don't have any more," said Darek, holding both hands up. "See?"

The dragon butted him playfully.

"All right, all right," said Darek. "I'll get more. Wait here." He turned and started toward the house. The dragon wobbled after him.

"No," said Darek, quickening his steps. "You stay."

"*Rrronk,*" said the dragon. It flapped its small wings and flew a few feet to catch up.

Darek stopped and stared at it, suddenly realizing what he'd done. He'd made friends with a dragon, an enemy of his people. Now what was he supposed to do?

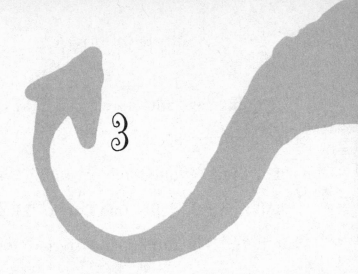

3

DAREK STRUGGLED TO CLOSE THE barn door, pushing the dragonling back in.

"You've got to wait here," he said. "And don't make a sound."

"*Rrronk,*" said the dragon.

"You don't understand," said Darek. "They'll kill you if they find you." He gave a final push, then pulled the door tight and lowered the latch. He could hear the orphan's muffled whimpers on the other side. He had to hurry or someone else might wake and hear.

Darek crept up to his room, dressed quickly, then tiptoed down to the back room where the weapons were kept. He slung his bow over his shoulder and strapped his quiver of arrows in place. On his way through the kitchen he filled a sack with supplies. It would be a journey of many days.

Suddenly he stopped and wondered, *What do dragonlings eat?* Perhaps such a young one would still need milk. He would have to bring along a female yuke. Dorlass, whose calf had been born dead, had milk to spare, but she would not nurse a dragonling. Darek packed a waterskin so he could feed the creature by hand.

Darek paused in the kitchen doorway and looked back. His stomach twisted into a knot. What was he doing, anyway? What would his father say? Risking his life to save a dragon? An enemy of his people? A dragon that *he* might even have to face one day on his own dragonquest? He could still turn back. It was not too late. Perhaps he should just let the creature be found and killed. After all, what more did a dragon deserve?

Darek walked slowly out to the barn. The soft hiccuping sound still came from inside. He opened the door, and the dragonling rushed out and rubbed happily against him.

"Thrrummm, thrrummmm, thrrummmm," it said.

Darek stroked its scaly head. "Why did you have to come here?" he whispered. Then he looked over at the lifeless body of the Great Blue. "I guess it wasn't your idea either, was it? Come then. I'll take you home, but after that I never want to see you again, understand?"

The dragonling thrummed happily. Darek took out another lump of sugar and let the orphan lick it from his hand. The sky was slowly growing lighter.

"Come on," said Darek, "we've got to go."

He led Dorlass out of the paddock. She was skittish around the dragonling. It kept running in and out between her legs, making her buck and jump while Darek was trying to get her saddle pack strapped on.

"Cut that out," said Darek, giving the dragonling a gentle kick.

"*Rrronk, rrronk, rrronk,*" it screeched, then it half ran, half flew back up to its mother's body and dove into her pouch.

Darek finished securing the saddle, then he led Dorlass over to the Great Blue. "Hey," he whispered, "come on out of there."

He saw a lump wiggle around in the pouch, but the dragonling did not appear.

"Come on, don't be such a baby," Darek coaxed. "I hardly even touched you."

The dragonling poked its head out. *"Rrronk,"* it said.

"I'm sorry," said Darek. "I thought dragons were tough."

He held out another piece of sugar, and the dragon crept slowly down again. Darek fed it and scratched its head until it was thrumming happily. "Some fighter you're going to make," he whispered.

Darek led Dorlass out to the road. The dragonling followed.

"You're going to have to move faster than that," said Darek, "if we're going to get to the pass before sunrise." He ran forward a few steps and then called to the dragonling. It flapped its wings and flew to catch up. Running and calling, running and calling, Darek managed to get to the foothills just as the first rays of the sun peeked over the mountaintops. Suddenly the little dragon turned back.

"Where are you going?" yelled Darek. He ran after the dragonling and grabbed it gently by the wings. It struggled to get away.

"*Rrronk,*" it squawked, "*rrronk!*"

It was staring back down the hill at the body of its mother.

Darek stroked its head.

"I know," he said. "It is *rrronk.*"

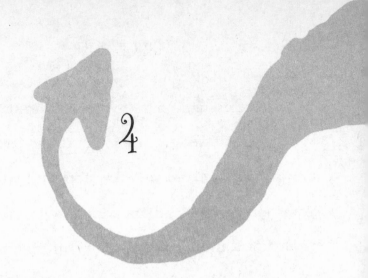

4

"I GUESS IF WE'RE GOING TO BE together awhile, I ought to give you a name," said Darek. "Are you a boy or a girl?"

The little creature didn't answer. It had spied an insect of some kind on the path, and it was all bent over, nose to the ground. Suddenly the insect bit it.

"*Rrronk, rrronk,*" it screeched, running over and shoving its head up under Darek's shirt.

"Will you get out of here?!" yelled Darek, giving

the creature a push and pulling his shirt back down. "I'm not your mother, and I don't have a pouch."

The dragonling lay down and curled itself around his legs.

"You're the sorriest excuse for a dragon I've ever seen," Darek said, peeling the orphan off his legs. Then he noticed its belly.

"You don't have a pouch either," he said. "That means you must be a boy."

"*Huf-uh, huf-uh,*" the dragonling sobbed, rubbing his nose with his forefoot.

"It's only a bug bite, for pity's sake," said Darek. "You have to toughen up. I'll give you a strong name, a powerful name. Then maybe you'll try a little harder to live up to it. I will call you Zantor, King of the Dragons."

Zantor whimpered and pushed his head under

Darek's arm. "Well," Darek said, "maybe you'll grow into it."

By evening Zantor was moving very slowly and stumbling often.

"It's been a long day for you, hasn't it?" said Darek. "We'll stop now and camp for the night."

Zantor moaned softly and nuzzled Darek's pocket.

"The sugar is all gone," said Darek. "But I'll get you some milk."

He set to work milking Dorlass, and when he had filled the waterskin, he held it up over the dragonling's head. "Drink," Darek said, letting loose a stream.

The milk squirted in Zantor's eyes and dripped off his nose, but he made no attempt to drink it.

"Didn't your mother teach you anything?"

said Darek. He opened the dragon's mouth with one hand and squirted the milk in with the other. Zantor started to sputter and choke. Darek stopped squirting, and the little dragon shook his head and spit all the milk back out.

"Look," said Darek, "it may not be your mother's, but it's all we have."

Zantor clamped his mouth shut and refused to drink.

Darek shrugged. Maybe dragons *didn't* nurse their babies. Maybe baby dragons ate regular food right away. It was worth a try. "I'll be right back," he said, shouldering his bow. "You wait here."

Darek didn't know whether Zantor understood or whether he was just too tired to move, but whatever the reason, he obeyed.

There were plenty of animals in the mountain forest, and Darek was a good shot. He quickly brought down a small glibbet* and carried it back to Zantor.

"There," he said, laying the animal at the dragon's feet. "Now eat." Darek sat down and laid out his own supper, some bread and cheese and a big cluster of barliberries.

Zantor sniffed at the glibbet, then he whimpered and began digging a hole. The next thing Darek knew, the dragonling had buried it.

"Hey," said Darek, "what are you doing? You can't save that. You have to eat it now. We're moving on in the morning."

Darek dug the glibbet up again, but when he turned around, he found Zantor happily munching on *his* barliberries.

*glibbet: a small weasel-like animal

"Well I'll be," said Darek. "You eat barliberries? What else do you eat?" He went into the woods and gathered all the herbs and nuts and berries he could find. Zantor gulped them greedily and followed him back to find more. At last they were both full, and Darek set about building a campfire. He gathered sticks and dry leaves, then he took out his flint and struck it against a rock. A spark flew out and landed on the leaves. Darek blew on it. It flared a moment, then died. Darek tried again. This time Zantor bent down, right next to him, staring intently. Darek blew on the spark. It sputtered and went out.

"Drat," said Darek. Then suddenly, *Whoosh!* A stream of flame shot by his nose. Darek jumped back. It was Zantor! Zantor was breathing fire!

In no time at all the campfire was burning

merrily. Zantor sat back on his hind legs, looking quite proud.

"Wow," said Darek. "That was pretty good. I didn't know you could do that yet."

Zantor thrummed happily, then curled up next to the campfire and went to sleep.

Darek stared at him. "You really are the strangest dragon I've ever heard of," he whispered, then he rolled his blanket out on the other side of the campfire and lay down.

The night was dark and damp, and the woods were full of strange calls and rustlings. Darek began to wish he were home in his own warm bed. He missed his family. Perhaps the little dragon felt lonely too, because before long Darek heard a soft scuffling, and then a small body nestled up against his own.

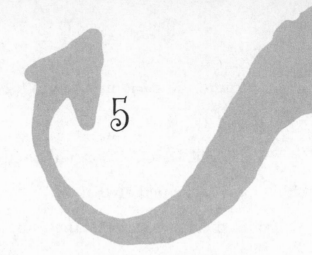

5

DAREK AWOKE TO FIND ZANTOR
still snuggled up beside him.

"Sleep well?" he asked.

The dragon thrummed and licked him on the
cheek.

"Will you cut that out?" said Darek. "You're
supposed to be tough, remember?"

Darek made himself a breakfast of bread and
barliberry jam while Zantor foraged in the woods,

obviously remembering all the places Darek had shown him the night before.

"Pretty smart, aren't you?" said Darek when the dragon came back. Zantor looked healthier already. His scales, which had been dull and greenish, were now turning a shiny peacock blue.

That day and the next two passed much like the first, except that Zantor grew stronger each day and was able to move more quickly. By the fourth day they were getting close to the Valley of the Dragons. Darek had never been there, but he had heard it described so many times around the campfire that he knew just what to look for.

"Won't be long now," he told Zantor. "You'll be home by afternoon." Zantor thrummed happily, and Darek wondered again if he somehow understood. Darek suddenly grew sad at the thought of leaving the dragonling behind. "That's what you came here for," he scolded himself angrily. "He's only a dragon, after all." But still, Darek worried. What would the other dragons think of Zantor, with his strange and gentle ways? Would they accept him, or treat him as an outcast? Or worse, would they kill him?

Darek and Zantor came upon the twin stones that marked the entrance to the valley, and Darek realized that they must proceed carefully. He tied Dorlass to a tree, then crept up to the top of a ridge to look out over the valley. Zantor scrambled up beside him.

"Get down, stupid," said Darek, throwing an arm around Zantor's neck and pulling him down.

"*Rrronk, rrronk,*" said Zantor, struggling to get free.

"Shhhush!" said Darek. Then he pointed down into the valley. "Look!"

Darek's heart pounded. For all his brave talk, he was unprepared for the size and number of creatures moving about below. Some of them lazed in the sun. Others waded in the river. Smaller ones butted heads together and tumbled like children in the dirt. There were caves cut into the mountains all around the valley, and occasionally a dragon would appear at the mouth of one and glide down on great wings to the valley floor. They were mostly Yellow Crested dragons, with a few Green Horned. Darek saw no Great Blues at all.

Zantor was staring at the scene excitedly.

"Is this your home?" Darek asked him. "Where are your kind?"

Zantor turned his head and looked toward the

mountain on the right, high up at the very largest caves. There was a sudden movement in the
shadows, and then a female Great Blue stepped
full into the sun. Darek knew it was a female from
the markings on her scales. She stood poised for
a moment on the edge, then lifted off and soared
out almost over their heads.

"Thrummmm, thrummmm, thrummmm," said
Zantor.

"Shhush!" whispered Darek, clamping a hand
over the dragonling's mouth. Darek stared up in
awe at the Great Blue. She was the most magnificent creature he had ever seen. The sun glinted
on her deep blue scales, making them sparkle
like the sea. Her wings stretched out silver and
shimmering against the pale blue sky. For all her
great size, she was sleek in the air, and when she

landed gracefully on the valley floor, she stood head and shoulders above the rest, like a queen.

Darek let go of Zantor's mouth. Zantor thrummed again, happily staring down at the Great Blue. Darek smiled and nodded.

"Yes," he said. "I think she would make you a fine mother."

6

GETTING THE GREAT BLUE TO adopt Zantor would be tricky. Zantor was not yet strong enough to fly down into the valley himself, and Darek wasn't about to *walk* him down. The best chance, he decided, would be to get the dragonling up to the Great Blue's cave while she was away. If she came home and found him in her nest, she might be more likely to accept him as her own.

Knowing what to do and doing it, however, were two different matters. The cave was high up on the mountainside. Climbing would be difficult, and worse, they would be in plain sight of the dragons. Darek decided that they'd make the climb at night, and then hide in the bushes near the mouth of the cave until the Great Blue went out in the morning.

Darek ate a large supper of cheese and milk and bread, and then topped it off with a generous helping of berries that he and Zantor had found. When the sun went down, Zantor started scuffling around, nose to the ground. He pushed a couple sticks together and started to blow on them.

"No, Zantor," said Darek. "No campfire tonight." He picked up the sticks and tossed them into the woods. Far back down the mountain pass, a bright flicker in the darkness caught his eye.

A campfire. Darek took a deep breath and let it out slowly. It was a search party, he was sure. His father and Clep and the others had come after him. He'd been so busy thinking ahead that he'd never thought back about the trail he was leaving. He guessed them to be about a day's journey behind him. He still had a chance to make his plan work, but there would be no second chances.

Darek sat down and looked at Zantor.

"I don't know if you understand me at all," he said, "but what I have to say is very important. You and I are going up there." He pointed to himself, then to Zantor, then to the cave. "We're going now. Tonight. Do you understand?"

Zantor stared where Darek pointed. *"Rrronk,"* he said.

"It *is* going to be *rrronk*," said Darek, "but we can make it. Just follow me, and be *quiet*." Darek put his hand around Zantor's mouth and held it shut to show him what quiet meant, then he moved off into the darkness. The dragonling followed.

Climbing was hard and slow. Zantor seemed better at it than Darek. He was lighter, for one thing, and his claws were good at finding niches to hold on to. Darek's hands grew sore and numb from the night chill. Several times he found himself wondering again why he was risking his life for a dragon.

Suddenly there was a piercing shriek. From a cave across the valley two dragons appeared. They roared and charged at each other. Their fiery breath lit up the night. Darek flattened himself against the rock, hoping the noise wouldn't awaken the Great Blue. Zantor whimpered. The two dragons, both Yellows, went on screeching for a while, then quieted down and went back into the same cave. Darek chuckled. "Perhaps they are husband and wife," he whispered to Zantor. "I've heard arguments like that back in the village."

Darek and Zantor edged onward. They had almost reached the cave when Darek felt himself slipping. He grabbed hold of a small bush and kicked out, madly trying to find safe footing. There was none. Darek's heart sank. His hands were so sore and tired he could hardly hang on. So this was how it was going to end? His father and Clep would find him dead at the bottom of the cliffs. What a fool he'd been.

Suddenly something tugged at the back of his neck, and Darek felt himself rising. He was dragged up and up until he was on firm ground again. Zantor landed beside him, breathing heavily.

"You?" said Darek. "You lifted me up, with those little wings?" Zantor seemed too tired to answer. He just laid his head in Darek's lap. Darek stroked it gently.

"Maybe you *are* growing into your name," he whispered.

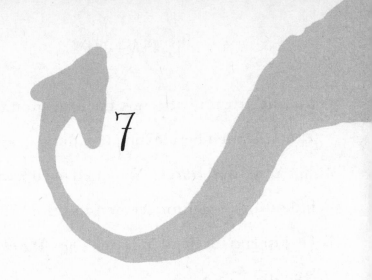

7

DAREK AND ZANTOR SPENT THE REST of the night in the bushes outside the Great Blue's cave. At the stroke of dawn, before it was even fully light, the Great Blue appeared. The whole valley quickly came to life. With great squawks and chatterings, dragons appeared at the mouth of every cave and crisscrossed down through the air. The Great Blue lifted off.

Darek sucked in his breath. "Well," he said,

"I guess this is it." He edged his way out of the bushes and into the cave, motioning to Zantor to follow. The cave was pitch-black inside, and Darek couldn't see a thing, but instantly the air was filled with a chorus of *rrronks*. Dragonlings! Zantor rushed past Darek back into the gloom, and the *rrronks* turned to excited thrummings.

Darek's eyes gradually adjusted to the darkness, and at last he could make out Zantor and two other slightly larger dragonlings tumbling merrily over one another. Darek smiled. He wished he could give Zantor a farewell hug, but he knew the smartest thing to do was to leave, fast. Just as he turned to go, a huge shadow darkened the mouth of the cave.

"*Grrrawk! Grrrawk!*" shrieked the Great Blue as she touched down on the outer ledge. Darek's blood turned to ice. She must have heard her babies cry and come back to check on them. If only he'd waited until she was out of earshot! Her great bulk filled the entrance. Darek whirled, looking for another passageway. There was none. These were not ordinary caves, he realized, just holes in the mountains hollowed out by the dragons' sharp claws.

"Grrrawk! Grrrawk!" the dragon screeched again. She glared at him, her green eyes glowing in the dark. Darek swung his bow off his shoulder and reached back for an arrow. With a trembling hand he fitted it to the string. There was only one unprotected spot, he knew, high up on the neck, just under the chin. She would lift her head just before battle. He would have one chance.

The dragon reared back. Flames shot from her mouth and lit up the cave. Darek took aim and—

Whomp! Darek took a hard blow to the back. He fell forward, the wind knocked out of him. He twisted in the dirt, gulping and sucking for air. When at last he could breathe again, he rolled over. Zantor stood behind him.

"Traitor!" Darek hissed, knowing even as he said it how foolish it sounded. Wouldn't he have done the same thing in Zantor's place? The Great Blue reared back and roared again, and Darek put his head down and waited for the end.

But instead of flames, or teeth, or claws, he felt only a small pressure. Zantor had lain down on top of him.

The Great Blue stopped roaring and started pacing back and forth, as if trying to decide how to deal with this strange turn of events. Her own dragonlings came over to her and made small mewing sounds. She picked them up and dropped them gently into her pouch. Then she came over and touched noses with Zantor. He whimpered and made little mewing noises too. She licked him tenderly, and he began to thrum. She picked him up and put him into her pouch as well.

Darek was glad, at least, that the dragon had accepted Zantor. Now it was *his* turn. With one claw the dragon ripped off Darek's quiver and tossed it over near his bow. In a mighty burst of flame the weapons disappeared. Darek cringed. With the same claw the dragon rolled him over. She sniffed him up and down and stared a long time into his eyes, then, to Darek's amazement, she hooked her claw through his shirt, picked him up, and dropped him into her pouch with the others.

Zantor nestled up against him. *"Thrrumm,*

thrrumm, thrum," he said. Darek let out a sigh of relief.

"I don't know what you told her," he said, "but thanks."

Darek was glad to be alive, but not at all sure what to expect next. He poked his head up. The Great Blue had turned and shuffled back out to the edge of the rock ledge. She plucked one of her dragonlings from the pouch and set him down before her.

"*Grok,*" she said. The dragonling wobbled for a moment on the edge, then fluttered out into the air. The dragon lifted out the second dragonling.

"Oh no." Darek groaned. "We *would* arrive just in time for flying lessons."

After the second dragonling was airborne, the Great Blue lifted out Zantor. Zantor stood timidly on the edge, his wings sagging. *"Rrronk?"* he said.

The mother dragon nudged him gently but firmly, and off he went. Darek closed his eyes, then opened one. Zantor flapped and fluttered for a moment, then straightened out and glided beautifully.

The next thing he knew, Darek found *himself* standing on the ledge. The drop to the valley below made his head swim and his knees feel like jelly. The Great Blue bent close and eyed him up and down. Then she turned him around and eyed him up and down again. Finally she snorted, picked him up, and put him back in her pouch.

The Great Blue lifted off and soared out over the valley. The wind whipped through Darek's hair and took his breath away. The ground raced by below him. He was flying! Suddenly Darek didn't even care if the dragons killed him in the end. The thrill of this moment made it all worthwhile.

The dragon made a surprisingly gentle landing. Zantor came running over, thrumming loudly, and jumped into the pouch with Darek. "Shush," said Darek, ducking down as far as he could. He was not sure the other dragons would accept him as readily as the Great Blue had.

All the dragons had moved into the forest— hunting, Darek imagined. The Great Blue and her two dragonlings followed. Darek peeked out. To his amazement, the dragons were not hunting at all. They were feeding on fruits and nuts and leaves, just like Zantor.

8

DAREK LAY BACK WITH HIS HEAD

resting on Zantor's round belly. The Great Blue

and the dragonlings were sleeping. All the dragons,

it seemed, returned to their caves for naps at mid-

day. Darek was drowsy too, after his long night, but

he was too excited to sleep. His mind was running

in leaps and bounds. If the Zorians could befriend

these dragons as he had, what a great help they

could be to one another. Darek had noticed that

food was not plentiful in the valley. Maybe that was why there were so few dragons left. The Zorians were great farmers. They could grow food for the dragons, and in return the dragons could help the Zorians in many ways. They could light fires. They could help plow the fields with their great claws. And *then*, there was the flying! Even a small dragon could probably carry four Zorians in its pouch at once. Journeys of several days could be made in hours! Darek could hardly wait to tell everyone of his discovery. He would probably become famous, maybe even go down in history. . . .

Darek finally fell asleep, dreaming of a bright new future for dragons and Zorians alike.

"Grrrawk!" Darek woke with a start. The Great Blue had jumped up and rushed, roaring, to the

mouth of the cave. Darek scrambled to his feet. He edged along the side of the cave and peeked out. There on a ledge just below the cave were his father, Clep, and the full Zorian hunting party.

The Great Blue roared again, head up, flames shooting out. Dragons began to emerge from the other caves. The Zorians formed a battle circle, shields and weapons pointing out. Darek's father, Clep, and several other men aimed up at the Great Blue.

"Father, no!" Darek shrieked. He ran out beneath the Great Blue's legs and waved his arms.

"Darek!" yelled his father. "Are you all right?"

"I'm fine," Darek shouted. He looked up at the Great Blue. "Wait, please!" he yelled to her. "Let me talk to them."

The Blue reared and tossed her head from

side to side. Darek turned back to the hunters. "Lower your weapons," he shouted. "You're making her nervous."

No one made any move to obey.

"Move aside, son," Darek's father called firmly.

"You don't understand," Darek insisted. "They're peaceful. They only fight to defend themselves. They're not the same as the dragons in the old days. They don't even eat flesh!"

Darek's words seemed to bounce off his father's stony face. *"Get out of the way, son!"* he repeated.

Darek turned to Clep. "Clep, you've got to make him listen," he begged.

Clep lowered his bow slightly and glanced uneasily at his father. "Maybe he's telling the truth," Darek heard him say. "Maybe we should listen."

"He is a child!" Darek's father yelled. "What

does he know of dragons? Raise your bow!"

Clep raised his bow again, but when he looked up at Darek, he seemed torn.

"Please!" Darek shouted again. "I *do* speak the truth." No one but Clep paid him any heed. Even Yoran's father, Bodak, turned a deaf ear to his pleas.

"*Grrrawk! Grrrawk!*" The Great Blue reared back. Flames shot out of her mouth.

"*For the last time,*" Darek's father yelled, "*get out of the way!*"

Darek stood trembling before his father's icy stare. All his life he had wanted nothing more than to make his father proud. Now he stood defying him. Why? Zantor bumped Darek's arm and whimpered. Darek looked down into the dragonling's gentle face and knew why. If killing without cause was what it took to be a man, he wanted no part of it.

The Great Blue roared and lifted her head. Darek saw his father narrow his eyes and train his bow on the dragon. *"Ready!"* he yelled. *"Aim!"*

Darek put his arms around Zantor and closed his eyes.

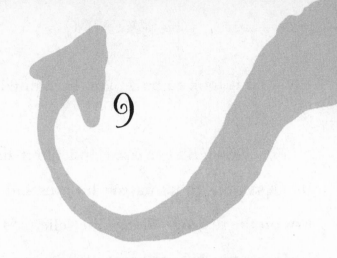

9

"STOP!"

The scream that split the air was piercing enough to be heard above the dragons.

Darek opened his eyes and stared. There, on the ridge beside the twin rocks, stood his mother. Zilah, Yoran's mother, was with her, and so were most of the other village women.

"Mother!" Darek called out.

Darek's father roared. "Are you mad, woman?

Get back, or the dragons will tear you to pieces!"

Darek watched, amazed, as his mother and the other women ignored his father's warning and began the dangerous climb toward the cave. The dragons, too, seemed stunned. Even the Great Blue stopped her roaring and thrashing and stood watching.

Darek glanced anxiously at the dragons as his mother and the others struggled for footings. Should the dragons decide to attack, they would be easy pickings.

"Get back, I tell you!" Darek's father repeated, but the women came on. At last Darek's mother reached the mouth of the cave, and Darek rushed into her arms. She hugged him tight, then looked uneasily up at the Great Blue.

"She won't hurt us," Darek said. "She's only protecting her babies."

Darek's mother nodded. She held up her hands. "I have no weapons," she told the Great Blue. Then she folded her arms around Darek again. "I am a mother, like you."

The Great Blue seemed to understand. She nudged Zantor back into the shadows.

"Take the boy and get out of there," Darek's father yelled, "while you've still got the chance!"

Darek's mother stepped to the ledge.

"It is not the dragons I fear," she shouted. "It is you."

Darek stared at his mother. Never in his life had he seen her speak so to his father. The other men stared too, and Darek's father's face grew as red as a burning ember.

"Perhaps I should leave you with the dragons, then?" he shouted.

The other women came up and stood behind Darek's mother.

"You will have to leave us all," she said. "We stand together. No longer will we let our sons be slaughtered for this cruel sport."

An angry murmur passed through the men, and Darek's father's eyes burned with rage. *"Sport!"* he shouted. "You call it *sport* to defend our people from their enemies?"

Darek's mother looked around at the great dragons on the cliffs. "If these creatures were truly our enemies," she said, "would I be standing unharmed before you now?"

Some of the men began to glance uncomfortably at one another.

"The old days are gone," Darek's mother went on. "We have suffered enough pain. Look at what you have done to Zilah. And to Marla and Deela and all the others whose sons are gone." Darek's mother pulled Darek close, and her voice began to tremble. "Look at what you would have done to me today."

Suddenly there was a cry, and Bodak, Yoran's father, dropped to his knees. He put his hands over his face, and his shoulders began to shake. He was weeping, Darek realized. A hard lump formed in his throat. He had never seen a man weep before.

There was a moment of stunned and awkward silence, and then, one by one, the men began to lower their weapons.

10

DAREK STOOD BY THE ENTRANCE TO the cave. A few ashes were all that remained of the pile of weapons. The dragons were still cautious, but they had allowed the villagers to return safely to the twin rocks. Darek was sure that friendship would come in time. He turned to Zantor. A great sadness filled his heart.

"You've grown already, little friend," he said.

"Soon you *will* be the greatest Great Blue of them all."

Zantor thrummed happily.

"You stay with your new mother now," Darek said, "and maybe we'll see each other again someday." Darek started toward the twin rocks. Zantor scuffled after him.

"No," said Darek firmly. "You have to stay."

Zantor stopped obediently and stood watching until Darek reached the ridge. *"Rrronk?"* Zantor cried out.

Darek looked back and waved, then he turned and hurried forward, blinking back tears. Just as he reached the group, there was a flutter and a thump, and then Zantor rushed up from behind and stuffed his head under Darek's shirt.

"Thrrummm, thrrummm, thrrummm," he said.

Darek giggled and pushed the dragonling away. "Will you cut that out?" he said.

The villagers laughed.

"Looks like you've adopted yourself a dragon," said Zilah.

Darek's father snorted. "No son of mine is going to play nursemaid to any dragon!"

Darek looked at Zantor. Clearly the dragonling wanted to come home with him, and Darek wanted nothing more. If only he could convince his father.

"Father . . . ?" he began.

His father eyed him suspiciously.

"I was thinking," Darek went on, his stomach fluttering, "the dragons could be our friends. They can light fires for cooking, they can help plow, they can even take us flying. I flew in the Great Blue's pouch. It was *wonderful!*"

In his growing excitement Darek did not notice his father's eyes growing rounder, and his face growing redder.

"Enough!" he boomed. "By the twin moons of Zoriak! What madness will you dream up next?" He whirled and stormed away.

Darek stared after him, his heart as heavy as stone. His mother put a hand on his shoulder and smiled.

"Change is never easy, my son," she said. "Your father has come a long way today. Give him time."

Zilah and Bodak stood nearby. Darek saw Zilah press Bodak's arm and whisper something into his ear. They murmured together, then Bodak nodded gravely.

"Your words are not easy to accept, young Darek," he said, "but they have much wisdom. Bring the orphan along. Zilah and I will care for him until your father is ready to listen."

Darek's heart leaped with joy, but he bowed his head humbly. "Thank you, Bodak," he said. "You honor me."

"And *I* honor my brother as well."

Darek looked up. Clep was standing before him, holding out the dragonclaw necklace. "This belongs to you," he said.

Darek was confused. "But why?" he asked. "You earned it."

Clep shook his head. "I just got lucky," he said. "It took true courage to do what you did today."

Darek's heart swelled with pride at Clep's praise. He took the prize and held it up. Somehow it brought him no joy now. He heard Zantor whimper beside him. Slowly he lowered his hand again. How could he return the gift to Clep without appearing ungrateful?

Clep seemed to understand. "Perhaps," he said quietly, "it really belongs to the dragons."

Together Darek and Clep dug a hole and buried the necklace between the twin rocks. Then they stood for a moment, side by side, looking out over the valley, peaceful and still now in the late afternoon shadows. Zantor wiggled in between them.

"*Thrrummm, thrrummm, thrrummm,*" he said.

A Dragon in the Family

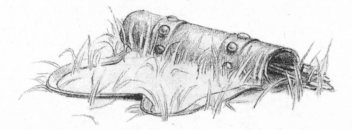

For Bobby, who fights a Red Fanged
dragon with a sword made of courage
and a shield made of love

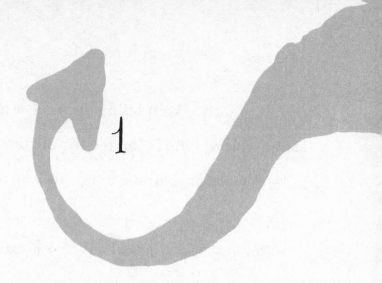

1

DAREK SAT ACROSS THE CAMPFIRE from his father, chewing but not tasting his food. It had been three days since their confrontation in the Valley of the Dragons, and still his father had hardly said a word to him. Would it be any different when they and the rest of their party reached home tomorrow? He glanced at his mother and his brother, Clep, and they each gave him a small reassuring smile. *Change takes*

time, his mother kept telling him. *How much time?* Darek wondered. He longed for the day when his father would gaze upon him with love and pride again.

"Rrronk," came a sad cry from back in the shadows.

Darek's father looked up from his meal and frowned.

"I'll quiet him," said Darek, jumping up. He lit a torch and picked his way through the forest to the spot where the dragonling had been tied. He saw the green eyes shining in the night before he could make out the small form huddled beneath a zarnrod tree.

"Rrronk, rrronk," came the cry again.

"It's all right, Zantor," Darek called softly.

"Thrrummm," the creature sang happily when

he heard Darek's voice. He strained against the chain that held him fast.

Darek stuck his torch in the ground and quickly unlocked the collar. The soft blue scales underneath were torn, and the flesh was rubbed raw from the dragonling's efforts to free himself.

"I'm sorry, Zantor," Darek whispered, stroking the small bony head. "This is Father's idea. He still finds it hard to trust you, though I keep telling him you're no threat to the yukes or anything else."

Zantor nuzzled Darek, and Darek smiled. "Come, little friend," he whispered. "Let's find you some supper."

Darek lifted the torch and led the way down the path as the creature fluttered and danced around him, happy to be free. They came upon a patch of barliberry bushes, and Darek sat on a rock and watched while Zantor fed hungrily.

Darek still had to pinch himself sometimes, so strange did it seem to be friends with a dragon. He remembered how startled he had been that night, after the last dragonquest, when he had found the newborn in its dead mother's pouch. He hadn't known what to do. Watching the little dragon now, though, Darek knew he had made the right decision. Returning Zantor to the Valley of the Dragons had led Darek to an important discovery. The dragons, which he had been taught to hate and fear all his life, were not what they appeared to be. Fierce only when threatened, they wanted nothing more than to be left alone to live in peace.

When Darek had shared this news with the members of the search party who came after him, the women had welcomed it—no more of their sons would have to die in the ritual dragonquests. But the men were harder to convince. It had taken Bodak, whose son, Yoran, had died in the last dragonquest, to turn the tide.

Zantor shuffled over and dropped a cluster of barliberries in Darek's lap. Darek smiled and scratched the little dragon under his chin.

"I still can't believe Father is letting you come home with us," Darek whispered. "But then, how could he object when Bodak and Zilah offered to take you in, even knowing that your mother killed their son?"

The dragonling snuggled down against Darek's leg, and Darek pulled a berry from the clump in his lap and chewed it thoughtfully. Why was Father still angry? he wondered. The other villagers in their party seemed to see the value of befriending the dragons. There would be no more fighting, no more killing. The dragons and Zorians could help one another in many ways. Most exciting of all, the dragons could take the Zorians flying! Darek's eyes shone as he remembered his own flight in the pouch of a Great Blue.

Then, as quickly as it had come, his joy faded into worry again. Darek's father was Chief Marksman, an important man in the village, soon to join the Circle of Elders. What if the elders felt as he did? What if they accused Darek of treason? Treason was a serious crime.

Crime! Darek suddenly sat up straight, eyes wide, heart thumping. No wonder his father was so upset. Now Darek understood. Darek had been so preoccupied by the dragonling, he hadn't stopped to think that he might be committing a crime. In

Zoriak, if a child under the age of twelve committed a crime, it was the father who suffered the punishment! And Darek was only nine. A heavy weight settled in his chest. Much as he loved the little dragon, he loved his father more. The last thing he wanted was to get him in trouble.

Darek heard a soft *"flubba bub bub bub, flubba bub bub bub."* He looked down to see the dragon curled up, gently snoring, his chin resting on Darek's foot. Darek sighed. His heart felt like the rope in a tug-of-war, pulled first this way, then that, until it was ready to snap.

"Why did my brother have to kill your mother?" he whispered to the sleeping dragon. "Why did your mother have to kill Yoran?"

"Flubba bub bub bub" was the dragon's only response, but Darek stared up at the night sky and

found his answer in the cold and silent stars. The killings had happened because the killings had always happened, and unless Darek could make a change, the killings would go on and on and on. . . .

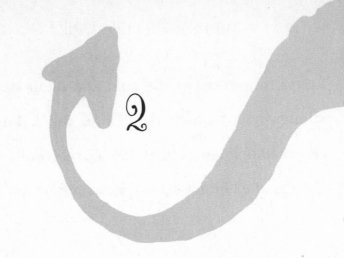

2

DAREK COULD HEAR THE VILLAGE bell clanging while he and the others were still some distance from town. The lookout had obviously caught sight of them. By the time they reached the bottom of the mountain pass, the village square was filled with people.

"Hooray!" the villagers shouted when they caught sight of Darek. "The boy has been found. The boy is well!" Then, on the heels of their cheers came another sound. A gasp of surprise swept through the crowd. "A dragonling!" Darek heard. "There's a dragon with him!"

Darek pulled in Zantor's chain, keeping him close. The crowd and the noise were making the creature skittish, and Darek wanted no problems. His father was already upset enough, staring straight ahead, stony faced as he strode along beside Darek. What was going through his father's mind? Darek wondered. What fate awaited them all?

"Darek! Darek!"

Darek whirled at the sound of the familiar voice. "Pola? Pola, where are you?" Darek searched for his best friend in the sea of faces around him.

"Here. Over here." A hand waved frantically, then Pola burst through the crowd and rushed up and threw his arms around Darek. "You're safe!" he cried.

"Yes, yes, I'm fine. . . ."

"What happened? They say you went to the Valley of the Dragons. They say—"

Suddenly Pola stopped talking and pulled back. He stared oddly at Darek. "By the twin moons of Zoriak," he whispered, "what happened to you?" He pointed at Darek's belly.

Darek looked down. In his excitement over see-ing his friend, he hadn't noticed that Zantor had somehow wiggled in between them and shoved his head up under Darek's tunic, making Darek look like a four-legged, blue-tailed beast that was about to deliver a baby.

Darek laughed in spite of his fear. "Will you

get out of there?" he whispered, pushing Zantor's head down and out.

"*Rrronk!*" cried the little beast. He ducked between Darek's legs and shoved his head up under the back side of the tunic.

Darek grinned, red faced, at Pola. "It's—it's a dragon," he stammered. "He—uh—thinks I'm his mother."

"A what?!" Pola took another step back.

"It's okay," Darek hurried to say. "He's harmless. See?" He gently pushed the dragon out from under his tunic again and coaxed him around front. "That's a good boy," he murmured, rubbing the knobby head affectionately.

"DAREK!"

Darek jumped, and the dragonling dived between his legs and up under his tunic again.

Darek turned in the direction of his father's voice and saw that the crowd had parted to let Darek's father, Yanek, pass. His father and the Chief Elder waited up ahead in the village square. "Bring the beast forward," his father yelled.

Darek gulped. "I gotta go," he whispered nervously to Pola. "I'll explain later." He hurried forward, dragging the baby dragon along behind.

3

DAREK STARED UP INTO THE STERN
eyes of the Chief Elder and blurted out the whole
story—how he had found the newborn dragon
and taken him back to the Valley of the Dragons,
how a Great Blue dragon had befriended them,
and finally, how he had placed himself between
the dragons and the Zorian rescue party in order
to avert a battle.

"The dragons let us go unharmed," Darek

ended breathlessly. "Don't you see? They didn't want to fight. They don't like to fight. They only fight to protect their young."

The Chief Elder's hard expression never wavered. If he found any of this news surprising, he gave no sign. All around them the villagers crowded close, murmuring in hushed tones and waiting for the Chief's reaction. Overhead the violet rays of the Zorian sun beat down. Beads of sweat began to trickle down Darek's neck and back.

Suddenly Darek felt something tickle between his shoulder blades. He twitched and tried to ignore it, but it came again. Zantor, still hiding under the back of Darek's tunic, was licking the droplets of salty sweat with his scratchy tongue. Darek twitched again and tried to hold back a giggle, but it was no use. The more he twitched, the more the little tongue flicked. At last Darek could stand it no more. He burst out laughing and crumpled up in a heap of hysterics, rolling and kicking on the ground, trying to get away from the tickly tongue. The more Darek laughed, though, the more Zantor seemed to think it was all a great game, and no sooner would Darek roll free than the little beast would pounce again, seeking out another bare patch of skin to tease. Round and round in the dust they rolled, laughing and thrumming, wiggling and tickling until at last they both lay still, too exhausted to move another muscle.

Darek lay on his stomach in the dirt, still giggling in little bursts and trying to catch his breath when he noticed the sea of boots and clogs around him.

"Uh-oh," he mumbled, remembering where he

was and why. He slowly rolled over and looked up.

The Chief Elder's eyes were hard as granite, and Darek's father's face was crimson, but, Darek noted with some relief, many of the other villagers were smiling.

"Rise!" the Chief's voice boomed.

Darek scrambled to his feet, and the dragon darted behind him and dived under his shirt again. The Chief Elder's face wrinkled in disgust. He turned to a pair of guards who stood nearby.

"Take the beast to the guardhouse," he said.

"The guardhouse!" Darek cried, his arms shielding the dragon. "No, you can't!"

The Chief Elder nodded to the guards, and they began to circle Darek.

"No. Please," Darek argued, circling too, trying to keep his body between the dragonling and the

guards. "You don't understand. He'll be terrified."

One of the guards lunged and grabbed Zantor by the tail.

"*Rrronk! Rrronk!*" the dragonling yowled, digging his claws into Darek's back.

"Ouch! Stop! Please! He's clawing me! Aaagh!"

The guard went on pulling, the dragon went on clawing, and Darek went on screaming until at last Darek heard his mother yell, "Yanek, for the sake of Lord Eternal, do something!"

Darek's father finally stepped forward and gave the guard a shove that sent him sprawling backward into the dust. Gasps of surprise rippled through the crowd, but Darek hardly noticed, intent on freeing himself from Zantor's frantic clutches. At last he coaxed the dragonling out from under his tunic.

"It's okay, Zantor. It's okay," he whispered. "I won't let them take you away." Zantor shivered and nuzzled his head against Darek's chest.

Darek's father went over and extended a hand to help the fallen guard to his feet, then he turned, his face crimson again, and bowed to the Chief Elder.

"A thousand pardons, Sire . . . ," he began.

"Silence!" The Chief Elder gestured to the guards. "Throw him in the guardhouse too!" he bellowed.

The guards grabbed hold of Darek's father, but before they could take him away, Darek's mother rushed up and linked arms with her husband. Bodak and his wife, Zilah, quickly joined them, then another woman and another man did as well. Soon the whole rescue party stood arm in arm. Darek's father seemed startled, and deeply touched.

"Sire," he said, his voice stronger now, "my son speaks the truth. Those of us who followed him to the Valley of the Dragons have seen it for ourselves. The time has come to talk."

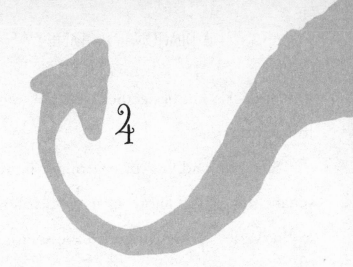

4

AN IMMEDIATE MEETING OF THE
Circle of Elders was called. Darek's father and
Bodak were commanded to attend.

"What do you think will happen?" Darek and
his brother, Clep, asked their mother as they
made their way home, trailed very closely by
Zantor.

"I don't know," she said simply. "We'll just have
to wait and see."

"But can't we do something in the meantime?" Darek begged.

"Yes," said his mother. "We can do the chores. Lord Eternal knows they've been left waiting long enough."

Zantor stepped on Darek's heel. Darek staggered a few feet, then regained his balance. He turned and glared down at the dragonling, who bumped smack into him again in his haste to catch up. All this togetherness was beginning to get on Darek's nerves. "Is it necessary to walk on my feet?" he snapped.

The little dragon stared up at him a moment in surprise, then—*thwip!*—out darted the forked tongue, planting a tickly little dragon kiss right on Darek's lips.

Darek rolled his eyes skyward, and Clep and

their mother burst out laughing. Darek couldn't help laughing too, which made Zantor do a happy little shuffling jig.

"That's the way," said Darek, nodding to the dragon. "Practice being cute. You're going to need all your tricks when Father comes back and finds we've brought you home with us."

"Well," said Darek's mother, "I don't see what choice we had, other than sending you off to live with Bodak and Zilah too."

Darek's smile faded and he sighed. "I fear Father will think that the better choice," he said.

Darek's mother slid an arm around his shoulders as they walked. "Don't you believe that," she said. "Not for a moment. Your father may be worried and confused, but he still loves you very much."

"Enough to put up with a dragon in the family?" asked Darek.

Darek's mother reached over and patted the little horn nubs on Zantor's head. "Yes," she said, "I think so . . . in time."

"In time?" Darek frowned. "But what are we to do *now*? Father will be back in a little while."

They had reached home, and Darek's mother pushed open the garden gate and looked over at the messy, neglected barnyard. "I think chores would be a *very* good idea," she said.

5

FORTUNATELY, MOST OF THE YUKES
had new calves, so they had not suffered for lack of
milking. The zok eggs had piled up some, though,
and were beginning to smell. The zoks squawked
and scolded as Darek and Clep reached into their
nests and gathered up the eggs.

"*Rrronk, rrronk,*" cried Zantor when the boys
carried two brimming basketfuls of foul-smelling
eggs out of the zok house. They carried them

down near the river, then went to get shovels. But by the time they had returned, Zantor had already dug a deep hole and pushed the eggs in. As the boys watched, he neatly covered the hole over again.

"Wow," said Clep. "He's pretty handy to have around."

"I told you," said Darek. "Imagine the things a big one could do. It could plow up a field in no time!"

"Yeah," said Clep thoughtfully. "Or dig irrigation ditches."

"Or help in the zitanium mines," added Darek.

"Or dig a swimming hole," said Clep, eyes shining. Darek and Clep had always dreamed of having their own swimming hole.

"Sure," said Darek as they picked up their

shovels and headed back to the paddock. "All we'd have to do is feed them."

"Feed them!" Clep wrinkled up his brow. "Did you happen to notice how big they get?"

"Of course I did. But with all their help we could easily raise enough food."

Clep still looked skeptical.

"Wanna see something else?" said Darek. He picked up a couple sticks and placed them on the ground. Immediately Zantor started shuffling around and nudging more sticks into the pile. When the pile was just the right size for a campfire—*whoosh!*—a stream of flame shot out of the little dragon's mouth and set it all ablaze.

"Wow," Clep repeated.

"That's nothing," said Darek, and he launched into the story of how he had flown in the pouch of a Great Blue, high above the Valley of the Dragons. Darek had already told Clep the story, several times in fact, on the journey back from the valley, but Darek could see that Clep was only just now beginning to believe it. Darek smiled, thinking how hard it would be for him to believe if it hadn't actually happened to him.

"It's like nothing you've done in your life before, Clep," he said wistfully. "They are the most magnificent creatures!"

Clep stared at Darek a moment, then looked away.

"What's wrong?" asked Darek.

"Nothing," said Clep.

"Yes there is. I can see it. Tell me, Clep. Please."

Clep kicked another stick into the fire and shoved his hands into his breeches. "It's just that . . . well, a

---

couple days ago I was a hero, a Marksman. Now I feel like a murderer. You've changed everything, Darek. I don't know what I am anymore."

SPLAT!

A zok egg came flying over the paddock wall and hit Darek square in the middle of the forehead.

SPLAT! SPLAT! A shower of rotten, rank-smelling zok eggs followed, pelting Darek, Clep, and Zantor.

"Traitors!" they heard. "Dragon lovers!"

Darek and Clep tried to protect themselves, but the eggs were coming too fast. The sticky yolks dripped in their eyes and blinded them. The smell made them gag. Then there was another sound, something between a *rrronk* and *grrrawk* followed by frightened yells and running footsteps, and the egg shower stopped.

Darek wiped the egg from his eyes and stared. Zantor was perched atop the paddock wall, wings spread, claws unsheathed, flames shooting from his mouth in a full dragon battle stance.

Darek and Clep raced to the wall in time to see a gang of young Zorian boys retreating over the nearest hill.

"Wow," said Clep, staring up at Zantor in awe. "I didn't think he had it in him. Did you ever see him act like that?"

Darek didn't answer. He was still staring at the hill.

"Darek," said Clep, "what's wrong?"

"I saw one of them," said Darek quietly. "It was Pola."

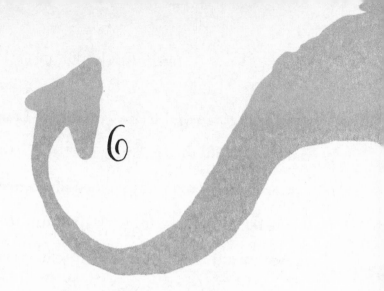

6

"TRY TO UNDERSTAND," SAID CLEP. "I probably would have done the same thing a week ago. The truth is, so would you."

Darek scrubbed the last of the rotten egg from his face, then bent down and ducked his head under the water again. Clep was right, he knew. Zorian boys spent years training for their dragon-quests. If someone had tried to tell him just last week that everything had changed, that he would never get to go on his, he would have been furious. He waded in toward the riverbank, shaking the water from his hair. Clep tossed him a drying cloth.

"Maybe you're right," Darek admitted, "but I never would have done anything like this to Pola. Never. He didn't even let me explain."

"Maybe it wasn't him," said Clep. "Maybe it was just somebody who looks like him from the back."

"Yeah," said Darek. "Maybe you're right." It made him feel better to believe that, even if it wasn't the truth.

Zantor still frolicked in the river, and the two brothers stood on the bank and watched him for a moment, deep in thought.

"It's all going wrong," said Darek quietly. "I thought everyone would be happy. I thought it would be so easy."

A DRAGON in the FAMILY

"I knew it wouldn't be easy," said Clep, "but it's the right thing to do."

Darek looked up at his big brother in surprise. "Do you really believe that?" he asked.

Clep nodded and clapped Darek on the shoulder. "Yes, I do." He smiled at his little brother's astonishment. "I even heard Bodak tell Father that he thinks you have the makings of a great leader."

"Bodak said that?"

Clep nodded, and Darek thought quietly for a moment. "What answer did Father make?" he asked.

Clep avoided his eyes. "There's the dinner bell!" he said quickly, seeming glad of a reason to change the subject. "Hurry and get dressed now."

Darek and Clep closed Zantor up in the barn with a pile of barliberries and a promise to return quickly, and to their surprise, he did not protest. He seemed to sense that this was home now. When they got to the kitchen, their father was already there. His face was grim and Darek's heart squeezed with fear. He longed to ask what had happened at the Circle, but his voice would not come out.

Clep started to ask, but a glance from their mother silenced him.

"Let your father have dinner," she said, "then we'll talk."

They ate in silence, Darek and Clep stealing worried glances at each other and at their father's somber face. At last Yanek pushed his plate away and lit his pipe. He sucked in deeply, then blew a long column of smoke from his lips.

"Is the beast with Zilah?" he asked.

Darek glanced nervously at Clep and their mother. "N-no," he stammered. "He wouldn't go with her. He's in the barn."

Darek's father nodded tiredly as if he'd expected as much, then went on smoking his pipe in silence. At last Darek couldn't stand the suspense any longer.

"What did the Circle decide?" he blurted out. "What was the vote?"

Darek's father took the pipe from his lips. "The Circle voted to put the beast to death," he said.

A cry of protest sprang instantly to Darek's lips, but his father held up a finger for silence. "I'm not through," he chided.

Darek nodded obediently, and his father went on.

"Bodak and I convinced the Circle that the beast deserves a trial," he said.

Darek's eyes opened wide in wonder. "You did?"

"Yes."

"But . . . why would you? I mean, I thought you didn't . . ."

Darek's father took another long puff on his pipe. "I'm a fair man," he said, then smiled at his wife and added, "if not always the most flexible one."

Darek's mother reached over and squeezed her husband's hand. "True on both counts," she said with a wink at Darek.

The great weight of the past few days began to lift from Darek's heart, but Clep still looked worried.

"What manner of trial do the elders have in mind?" he asked.

"Simply this," Yanek answered. "The beast can live among us until the first sign of trouble."

"And if there *is* trouble?" Clep inquired.

Darek's father glanced at the faces of his wife and sons, then lowered his eyes. "*Then* he will be put to death," he said quietly, "and so will Bodak and I."

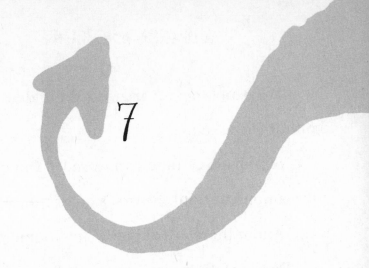

7

DAREK SAT ON A BALE OF ZORGRASS watching Zantor try to perch on a yuke stall like a zok. It was obvious that the dragonling was doing his best to make Darek laugh, but Darek's heart was too heavy. How could this be happening? he wondered. How could an act of love and caring get twisted into such a nightmare?

"It isn't fair," he cried out. "It just isn't fair!"

"What isn't fair?"

Darek turned and saw his father standing in the doorway. Darek turned away again, fighting with all his might to hold back the tears. "Nothing," he said softly.

There were footsteps, and then Darek felt a hand on his shoulder.

"Mind if I sit down?"

Darek looked up, and then the tears stung his eyes and slid down his cheeks. "Oh, Father," he whispered. "I'm so sorry."

Darek's father sat down next to him, leaned his elbows on his knees, and clasped his hands together tightly.

"No, son," he said. "I am the one who is sorry."

"You?" Darek started to protest, but Yanek held up a finger to silence him.

"Hear me," he commanded.

Darek wiped his eyes and nodded.

"I have treated you badly," Yanek went on. "In truth, the anger I have shown to you these past few days was really anger and contempt for myself."

Darek stared at his father in astonishment. "But why?" he asked.

Yanek rubbed his forehead tiredly. "Because in my heart I have known for a long time the truth about the dragons, and I have denied it."

Darek's mouth fell open in disbelief, and Yanek shook his head as if irritated with himself. "In the old days," he went on, "when the Red Fanged and Purple Spiked dragons roamed the valley, our fathers were great warriors. Their skills protected their families. Their deeds of valor gave them places of honor in our society. They fought until the Reds and Purples were gone."

Yanek fell silent, and Darek stared at him in confusion. "Then what happened?" he asked.

Darek's father sighed. "What is a warrior without a war?" he asked. "Somehow all dragons became the enemy. Green Horned, Yellow Crested, Great Blue . . . What matter that their kind never bothered our villages? What matter that they had not even a taste for flesh? When a man wants to be a hero, he needs a foe to vanquish."

Darek looked over at Zantor, who had finally accomplished the task he had set for himself and sat staring at them proudly like an oversize blue zok. The sight was so comical that Darek might have laughed if he hadn't felt so heartsick.

"Then it's all been a lie," he said. "All the training, all the battles, all the deaths . . ."

Yanek nodded slowly. "Yes," he said, "and that's why what you have done is so dangerous."

"Dangerous?" Darek repeated.

"Yes," said his father. "I'm afraid our whole society is built around this lie, and those who have gained the most from it will fight hardest to keep the truth a secret."

"You mean . . . the Circle of Elders," said Darek.

"Yes," said Yanek.

"But how?" asked Darek. "How can they fight this?"

"The same way they always have, my son. By making the lie appear to be true, so true that they can believe it themselves."

"How can they do that?"

There was a sudden commotion out in the

yard, followed by the sound of many voices raised in anger.

Darek's father stiffened. "I fear we are about to see how," he whispered.

"Yanek!" a voice boomed. "Yanek of Zoriak, come forth!"

"Silence!" the Chief Elder boomed. "Where are you hiding the beast?"

"The beast?" said Darek, so frightened that for a moment he couldn't think what the Chief Elder meant.

"Don't play the fool!" the Chief bellowed. "We know . . ."

He never had to finish his sentence, for at that moment a zok strutted out of the barn, and right behind it strutted Zantor, doing the silliest zok imitation Darek had ever seen.

No one was amused.

"He's there!" came a panicky cry. "Watch out! Seize him!"

Shrieks of fear rang out on all sides, and before Darek knew what was happening, Zantor was

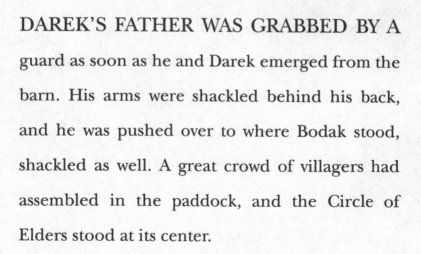

8

DAREK'S FATHER WAS GRABBED BY A guard as soon as he and Darek emerged from the barn. His arms were shackled behind his back, and he was pushed over to where Bodak stood, shackled as well. A great crowd of villagers had assembled in the paddock, and the Circle of Elders stood at its center.

"What's wrong?" Darek cried. "What are you going to do with my father?"

snagged in a chain-mail net. A zitanium cage was rolled up, and the little creature was tossed inside.

"*Rrronk! Rrronk!*" he cried out.

Now that the dragonling was safely locked up, a group of children began to tease and taunt him, poking him with sticks and tossing stones into the cage. Zantor's *rrronks!* became shrill *grrrawks!* He unsheathed his claws and began charging at the bars, arrows of flame shooting from his mouth.

"Do you see?" screamed a hysterical mother to the elders. "Is it not as I said?"

The Chief Elder nodded slowly. His face was stern, but it was obvious that he was well pleased with the events that were taking place before him.

At that moment Darek's mother burst out of the house, followed by Clep.

"What's going on?" she cried, staring wildly at the scene before her. "What's happened?"

"I fear, Madam," said the Chief Elder, "that the beast has attacked a group of boys unprovoked. Friends of your son, I believe."

Darek's eyes widened. "That's a lie!" he shouted.

"A lie?" The Chief Elder turned toward Darek. He smiled slowly and snapped his fingers. "Bring the boys here," he called over his shoulder. Two mothers came forward with two boys Darek knew, but not well.

"See for yourself," said the Chief.

The boys turned, and Darek saw that their clothes were scorched and their hair singed. The chief gave Darek a smug look.

"They're not friends!" Darek cried. "They

tried to hurt me and Clep. Zantor was just defending us."

The Chief turned a deaf ear to Darek's pleas. "Take the prisoners to the council house!" he shouted. "Let the trials begin!"

9

DAREK STARED HELPLESSLY AS
Zantor continued to thrash and roar in his cage
outside the council house. Now and then the
dragonling made a new sound, an earsplitting
eeeiiieee! If found guilty, Zantor would be the lucky
one, though. He would simply be target practice
for the archers. Darek's father and Bodak would
be burned at the stake.

Darek's mother and Zilah tried desperately to

convince the waiting villagers that Zantor, Yanek, and Bodak were innocent, but the group of boys continued to hold to their story of terror, and sympathy was on their side.

Darek and Clep paced nervously.

"I've got to *do* something," said Darek. "I can't just wait here like this."

"Haven't you done enough already?" Clep snapped.

Darek stopped pacing and stared at his brother. "Are you blaming me, Clep?" he asked quietly.

"Yes . . . No." Clep put his hands over his face. "I don't know what to think anymore. I just want it to be a bad dream. I want to wake up and find out that it's just an ordinary day and we're all going fishing like we used to, me and Yoran, and you and Pola—"

"Pola!" Darek grabbed Clep by the shoulders and stared into his eyes. "Pola was with them, remember? Pola knows the truth!"

Clep stared back for a moment, then shook his head. "You're not sure of that," he said, "and even if he was with them, what makes you think he'll tell the truth?"

Darek stared over Clep's shoulder at Zantor. "He'll tell," he whispered. "I'll *make* him tell."

Darek found Pola out behind his house, shooting arrows aimlessly into the air.

"Pola!" he shouted. "Pola, we've got to talk!"

Pola glanced over his shoulder at Darek, frowned, and looked away again. He loosed another arrow, watching its lazy flight.

"Pola, listen to me!" Darek ran up behind

his friend, grabbed his arm, and whirled him around.

"Hey," Pola growled, pulling his arm free. "Leave me alone."

"No!" Darek shouted. "You've got to help me."

"Help you do what?" asked Pola sullenly.

Darek stared at him. "Haven't you heard?" he asked. "Don't you know?"

"Know what?" asked Pola.

"They're trying my father," shouted Darek, "and my friend Zantor." Darek narrowed his eyes. "You know," he added dryly, "the fierce dragon who attacks young boys unprovoked."

Pola's eyes widened, then he looked away.

"I—I don't know what you're talking about," he said.

"No?" Darek grabbed the hat from Pola's head

and clutched a handful of singed hair. "Then how did you get this?"

Pola said nothing.

"Answer me, Pola!"

"I—I never meant to hurt your father," mumbled Pola. "I just wanted to get the dragon."

Darek let go of Pola's hair and handed him his hat. "Why?" he asked angrily. "What did the dragon do to you?"

Pola whirled away and slammed his bow to the ground. "It doesn't belong here!" he shouted. "It changes everything, don't you see? All the training, the matches, the tournaments, all the games of skill we've played all our lives! None of them matter anymore."

Darek stared at the bow lying between them on the ground. He wanted to hate Pola, but he couldn't. He understood Pola's feelings too well. In his heart he knew he would have felt the same way once.

A great clamor of voices rose up, carried on the wind from the village square. Time was running out. Darek had to win Pola to his side now. He grabbed up the bow and found an arrow that lay nearby. He fitted the arrow to the string and surveyed the meadow. Far away on the opposite side stood a young purple sapling. Reaching it would be quite a stretch, but Darek had to try. He tilted the bow up and let fly. He watched, holding his breath as the arrow arched out high over the meadow, then dropped slowly and . . . struck! Praise Lord Eternal. His aim was true.

Darek lowered the bow and looked at Pola. His friend was envious of the shot, he could tell.

"Here," he said, holding out the bow. "Match that."

"What?"

"Match it," Darek repeated.

"Why?" asked Pola, narrowing his eyes.

"Because you want to," said Darek. "Admit it. Whether you ever fight a dragon or not, you *want* to shoot, because you want to prove you're as good as me. That's where the fun lies, Pola. In the competition, not the killing. Match it. I dare you."

Pola stared at Darek a long time, then silently took the bow and pulled an arrow from his quiver. Slowly he turned, fitted the arrow to the string, and took aim. Darek held his breath again as the arrow arched out over the meadow, going higher, higher, then lower, lower, and . . .

10

DAREK WAS PREPARED FOR A GUILTY verdict, but he was not prepared for the sight that greeted him when he and Pola reached the square. The executions had begun! Yanek and Bodak were lashed to their stakes, and archers were lining up in front of Zantor's cage.

"Stop!" Darek shrieked as he and Pola tried to push their way through the crowd. "Stop! It's all a mistake!"

No one listened. No one cared. Everyone was too busy watching the show, shouting and jeering.

"Stop!" the two boys cried together. "Somebody listen, please!" Darek pushed and shoved at the crowd, but he was making no headway. He pushed at a big man who pushed him back and sent him sprawling in the dust. Darek scrambled to his feet again, grabbed a rock, and motioned for Pola to follow. He got as close as he could to the platform where the village bell sat, then let the rock fly.

CLANG . . . ANG . . . ANG!

All heads turned as Darek hoisted himself up onto the platform and pulled Pola up too.

"Stop!" Darek yelled. "This is all a mistake! We've got to stop the executions now!"

The Chief Elder gave a signal, and the guards

touched flaming torches to the piles of brush that circled Yanek and Bodak.

"NO!" Darek cried. "These men are innocent!"

"It's true," Pola shouted. "I was among the boys." He turned so people could see his singed hair, then turned back and hung his head in shame. "We attacked Darek and Clep," he went on. "We provoked the beast!"

Mouths dropped open and a hush fell over the crowd. Then, "He's lying!" someone shouted.

"Aye! Aye!"

"No!" Pola cried. "It's the truth." He scanned the crowd before him. "Malek!" he said suddenly. "Dorwin!" He pointed to the two boys who had brought the charges. "Tell them! This has gone too far."

All eyes turned toward the two boys. They

stared at each other uncomfortably for a moment, then slowly nodded and hung their heads. The crowd gasped.

"Don't you see?" shouted Darek. "The only lie is that the dragons are our enemies! Do they attack our villages? Do they raid our herds? No! They fight only when we attack them, only when they are provoked!"

Darek could see that he had the attention of the crowd now. He pointed to where his mother and Zilah stood. "Zilah's son is dead," he said, "and so is my mother's brother. How many others of you have lost sons, brothers, husbands, or fathers?"

People murmured together, then a hand went up, followed by another, and another. Darek watched until almost everyone had a hand in the air. "Look!" he shouted. "Turn your heads and *look,* and then decide. . . . How many more must die for the sake of a lie?"

Heads swiveled, then hands were slowly lowered and shoulders sagged in sorrow. The silence was heavy, broken only by Zantor's shrill screams. Then came another tortured cry.

"Aa-a-gh!"

"Yanek! Bodak!" someone yelled. "Water! Hurry!"

The crowd came to life, and people flew in all directions, but time was running out. Bodak and Yanek writhed in agony as flames licked at their legs.

"Eeeiiieee!" shrieked Zantor. *"Eeeiiieee!"*

The pitch of Zantor's shrieks became so high that people in the crowd began to clasp their ears and cry out in pain. Then, as Darek watched in astonishment, Zantor's cage shattered like a crystal

shell, and the little dragon rose up into the air. He fluttered over and dropped down into the ring of flame that surrounded Darek's father. A moment later the dragonling rose up again, tiny wings pumping furiously. Darek's father's great limp body was clutched tightly in his claws.

Darek's father and Bodak sat sipping hot glub from steaming mugs, their bandaged feet propped up on chairs. Zantor was curled up in exhausted sleep between them, and Yanek reached down and stroked his small head affectionately.

The little dragon stirred. *"Thrrummm,"* he mumbled tiredly.

Bodak smiled. "You know, Yanek," he said, "I still can't quite believe I'm sitting here."

Yanek nodded and looked over at Darek. Love

and pride glowed in his eyes. "Aye," he said, shaking his head in wonder, "neither can I, but I guess when you have a son who has the makings of a great leader, anything is possible."

Darek smiled back, warmed by his father's words, but a little bit frightened, too. Leadership, he had discovered, could be a pretty scary business. Maybe he *would* be a leader someday, but for now he just wanted to be a boy again, a boy with a dragon in the family.

Dragon Quest

To my brother, Richard, with love

Prologue

WHEN DAREK'S FATHER AND BROTHER
went off with the other hunters on a dragonquest,
Darek wished with all his heart that he could have
gone too. Like all the other boys his age, Darek
dreamed of being a hero and fighting a dragon.
When the hunters returned with a slain Great
Blue, the largest and fiercest of all dragons, the
villagers gave them all a hero's welcome. Darek
thought the hunters were heroes too, until he

found a baby dragon hiding in the dead Great Blue's pouch. The dragonling was so small and frightened that Darek felt sorry for it and decided to take it back to the Valley of the Dragons. There, Darek made a startling discovery. Dragons were peace-loving creatures and killed only in self-defense.

Darek gave the baby dragon a powerful name, Zantor, and brought it back to his village. But the other Zorians did not welcome the dragonling. They nearly put Zantor to death, and Darek's father, too! With the help of his best friend, Pola, Darek finally managed to convince the villagers of the truth about dragons, but it was almost too late. The executions had begun! At the last moment, young Zantor proved that he was worthy of his name, saving himself and Darek's father.

Now Darek, Pola, and Zantor are the heroes, and all seems peaceful at last, but Darek's father is still worried. "Such things are not always as simple as they seem," he warns.

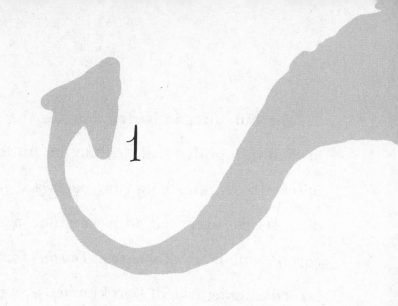

1

DAREK POINTED A STICK TOWARD the sky. He swung it in two wide circles, then slowly lowered it until its point touched the ground. Above his head Zantor soared, following the pattern Darek had traced in the air. The dragonling circled once, then twice over the paddock. Then he swooped down for a landing.

"Hooray!" Darek shouted. He and his best friend, Pola, clapped excitedly. "That was perfect!"

The little dragon barreled across the field in his funny, lopsided gait. Joyfully he hurled himself at Darek, knocking him backward into the dirt. Darek squirmed with laughter as Zantor covered his face with kisses. *Thwip! Thwip!* The forked tongue tickled! Darek pulled a sugar cube from his pocket and tossed it a few feet away. The dragon scuffled after it, and Darek got to his feet and dusted himself off. Pola was laughing, but he wasn't the only one, Darek realized. He turned and saw that he, Pola, and Zantor had an audience. A group of village children were hanging over the paddock fence.

"Zantor! Zantor, come here!" they cried, reaching out eager hands. When Zantor waddled over to play, the children shrieked with delight. "Let me pet him first!" one cried out. "No, me! No, me!" the others shouted.

Darek frowned. He was pleased, of course, that the villagers had finally accepted Zantor. For a time it had seemed that they wouldn't even let him *live*. But Zantor had proven to all that he was both peaceful and courageous, and now they were willing to let him live among them. In fact, Zantor had become so popular lately that Darek seemed to be forever fighting for the dragonling's attention. Darek was the one who had found Zantor, after all, and brought him to the village. Why should he have to share him now with people who hadn't even wanted him at first? It didn't seem fair.

"Hey." Pola nudged Darek in the ribs. "Look who's here."

Darek looked where Pola had nodded. A taller girl had joined the other children. Her long dark hair fell over her shoulders as she reached out and scratched the horn nubs on Zantor's head.

Zantor buried his face in the girl's shining hair and thrummed happily. Darek's frown deepened. "Rowena," he said with a groan.

Pola grinned. "I think she likes you," he said. "She's always hanging around lately."

"It's not me she likes; it's *him*," Darek said. "Besides, who cares?"

"She's awful pretty," Pola teased.

"Yeah," Darek agreed, "and she's awful head-strong, stuck-up, and spoiled."

Pola laughed. "Maybe you'd be headstrong, stuck-up, and spoiled too if *your* father was Chief Elder."